The Elephants' Ears

written by **Catherine Chambers**
illustrated by **Caroline Mockford**

Barefoot Books
Step inside a story

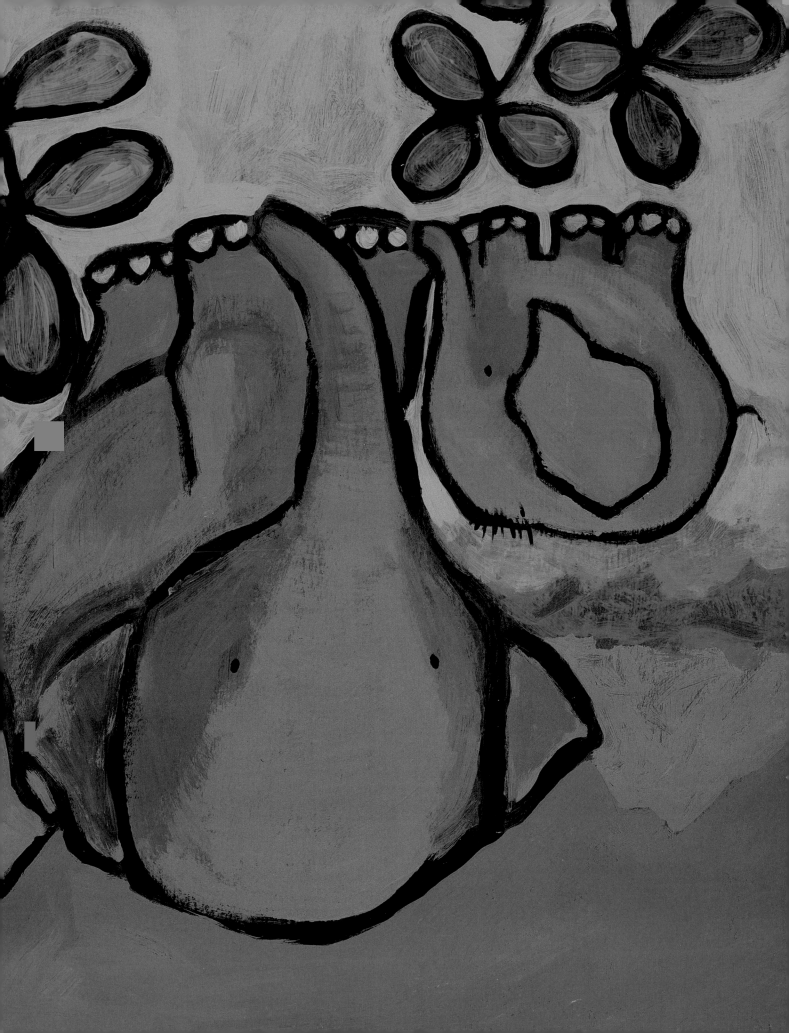

At the foot of a snow-covered mountain, there lived a mother elephant. She had two young calves, a boy called Palo and a girl called Mala.

And they looked almost the same, except that Palo had small, neat ears and Mala had wide, flapping ears.

Palo and Mala played happily all day long. Palo shared mangoes with the baboons in the forests at the foot of the mountain. Mala ran with the zebra that raced across the hot, dry grasslands.

In the evening, as the shadows grew longer, Palo and Mala made their way home. Mother Elephant found them a safe place to rest for the night.

There, Mala tossed and turned, while Palo snuggled down and fell fast asleep.

The young elephants grew
fast. They stopped playing with
the animals that roamed around
the mountain. It was soon time
for them to go out into the
world and live their own lives.

Mother Elephant watched them closely, shaking her head sadly and whisking her tail. "Oh, Palo and Mala! You are so very different from each other," she said. "I just don't know what kind of life will be best for you both."

"Aaaaaaa," crooned Mother Elephant, nodding her head at Palo. "You with your neat little ears and soft, gentle ways. You will be happiest in a place where you can work hard and live peacefully."

"Aaaaoooo!" she trumpeted, shaking her head at Mala. "You with your grand, flapping ears and wild, wild ways. You will be happiest in a place where you can feel free."

Mother Elephant rocked from side to side, thinking hard. She watched Palo collecting piles of leaves and bark for the family's lunch, while Mala rolled happily in a muddy pool.

Then, Mother Elephant
looked up and saw a tiny black
dot circling the mountain top. It
was the giant black eagle, kind
and wise. Now Mother Elephant
knew exactly what to do. She lifted
her trunk and roared, "Oh, Queen
of the Mountain, please help me to
find a place for Palo and Mala in
the great, wide world."

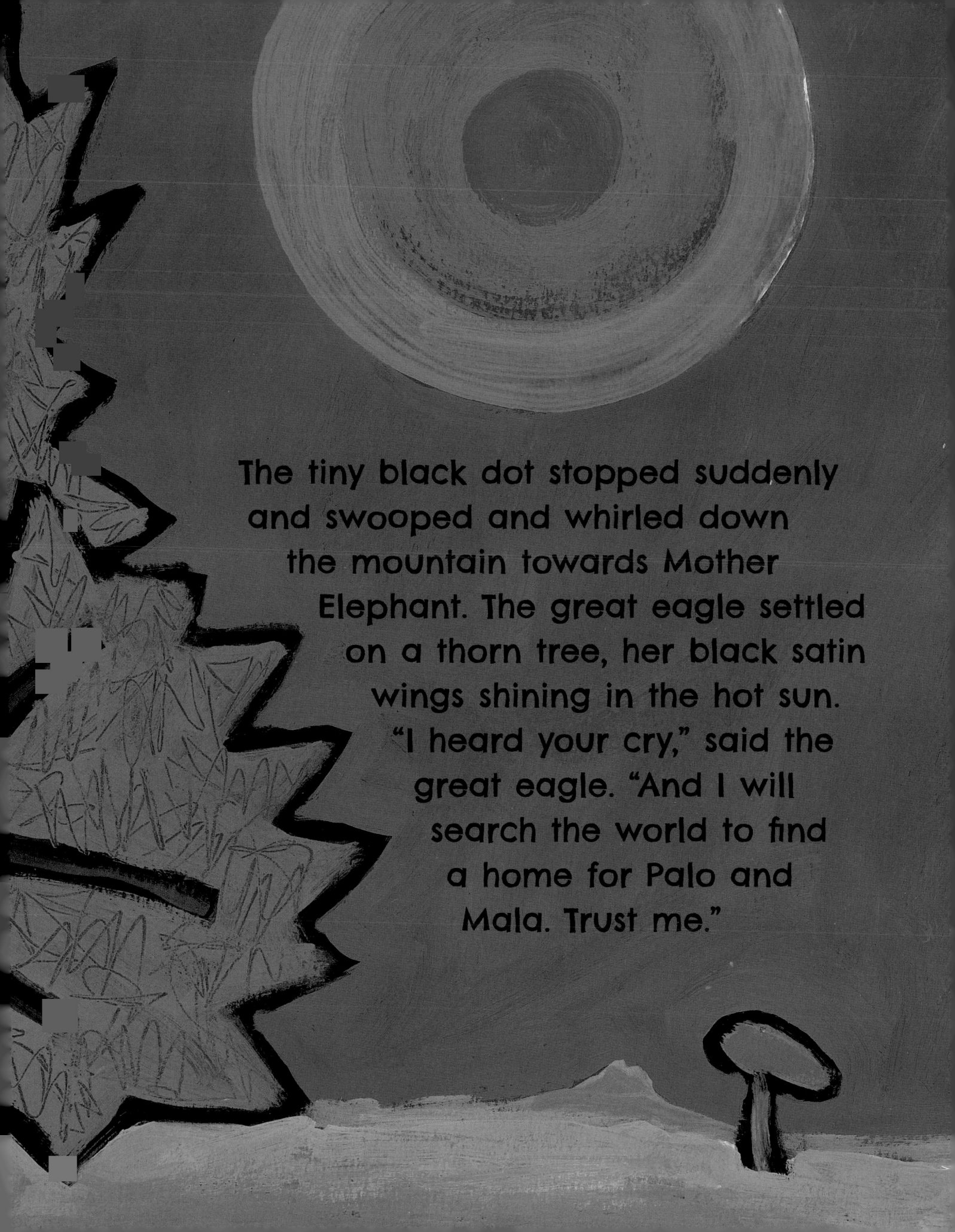

The tiny black dot stopped suddenly
and swooped and whirled down
the mountain towards Mother
Elephant. The great eagle settled
on a thorn tree, her black satin
wings shining in the hot sun.
"I heard your cry," said the
great eagle. "And I will
search the world to find
a home for Palo and
Mala. Trust me."

She flapped her wide wings, blowing the dust into a billowing red cloud. Then she began to circle the earth.

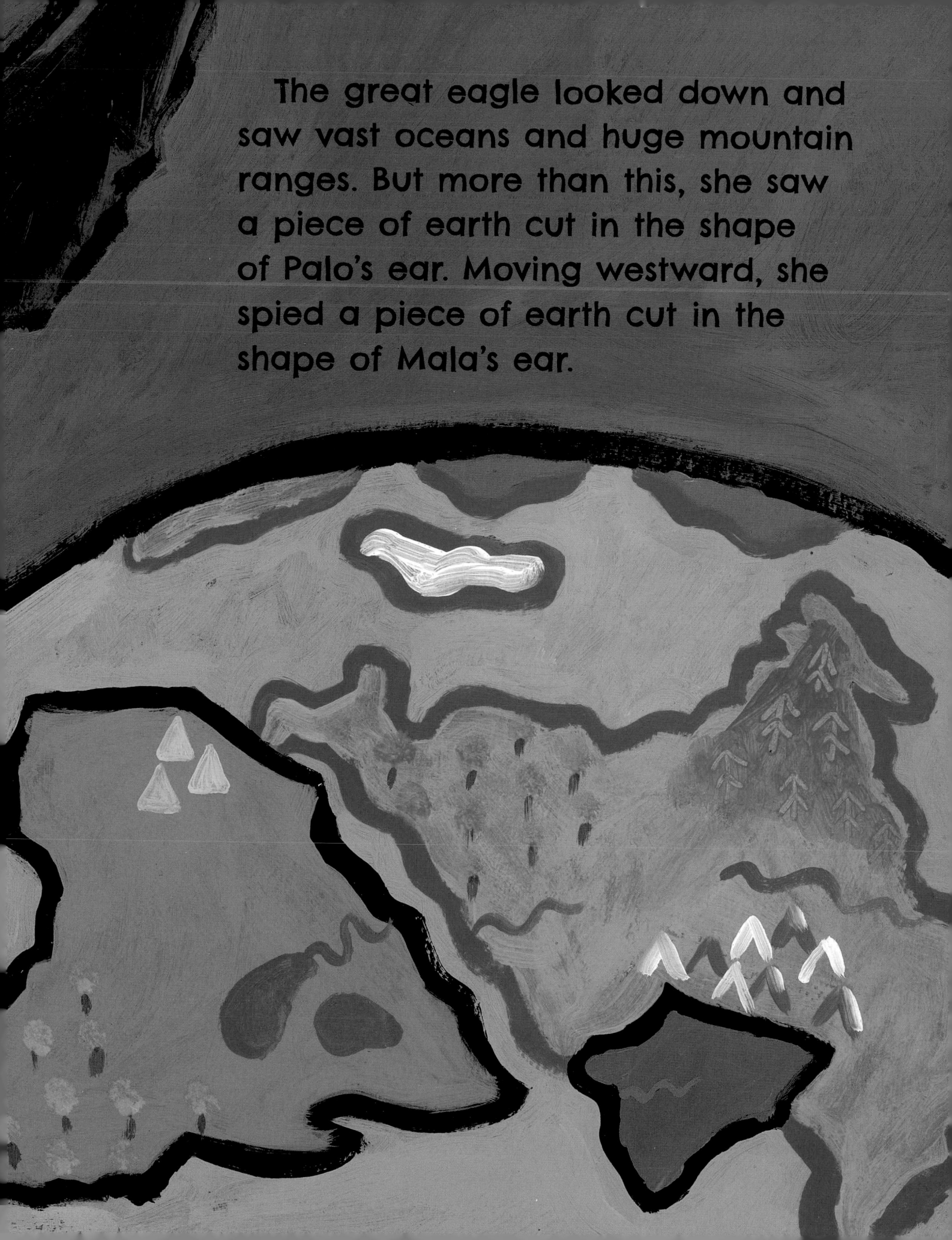

The great eagle looked down and saw vast oceans and huge mountain ranges. But more than this, she saw a piece of earth cut in the shape of Palo's ear. Moving westward, she spied a piece of earth cut in the shape of Mala's ear.

With great excitement, the wise eagle made her way back to the mountain. As she flew, she called upon a white egret and a pink flamingo to follow her. Sitting once more in the thorn tree, the Queen of the Mountain called Palo and Mala to her side.

"Now," she said. "I have searched the whole earth. But I haven't found a place where Palo and Mala can live together." Mother Elephant shook her head sadly. "But," continued the wise eagle, "I have found two homes where each of them can find happiness."

The great eagle turned to Palo. "Now, Palo," she said. "I have found the perfect place for you. Follow the white egret. He will lead you there."

She turned to Mala. "Now, Mala," she said. "I have found the perfect place for you. Just follow the pink flamingo. He will lead you there."

Mother Elephant knew that it was
time for Palo and Mala to leave their
home. She wrapped her long trunk
around them and held them both tight.

"Goodbye, Palo," she said. "Be fair and wise. Goodbye, Mala. Be kind and strong." And with a loud, loud trumpet, Mother Elephant finally let them go.

Palo walked and
walked until the white
egret spied land in
the shape of Palo's ear.

It was India.
There Palo stopped.

Mala walked and walked
until the pink flamingo spied
land in the shape of Mala's ear.

It was Africa.
There Mala stopped.

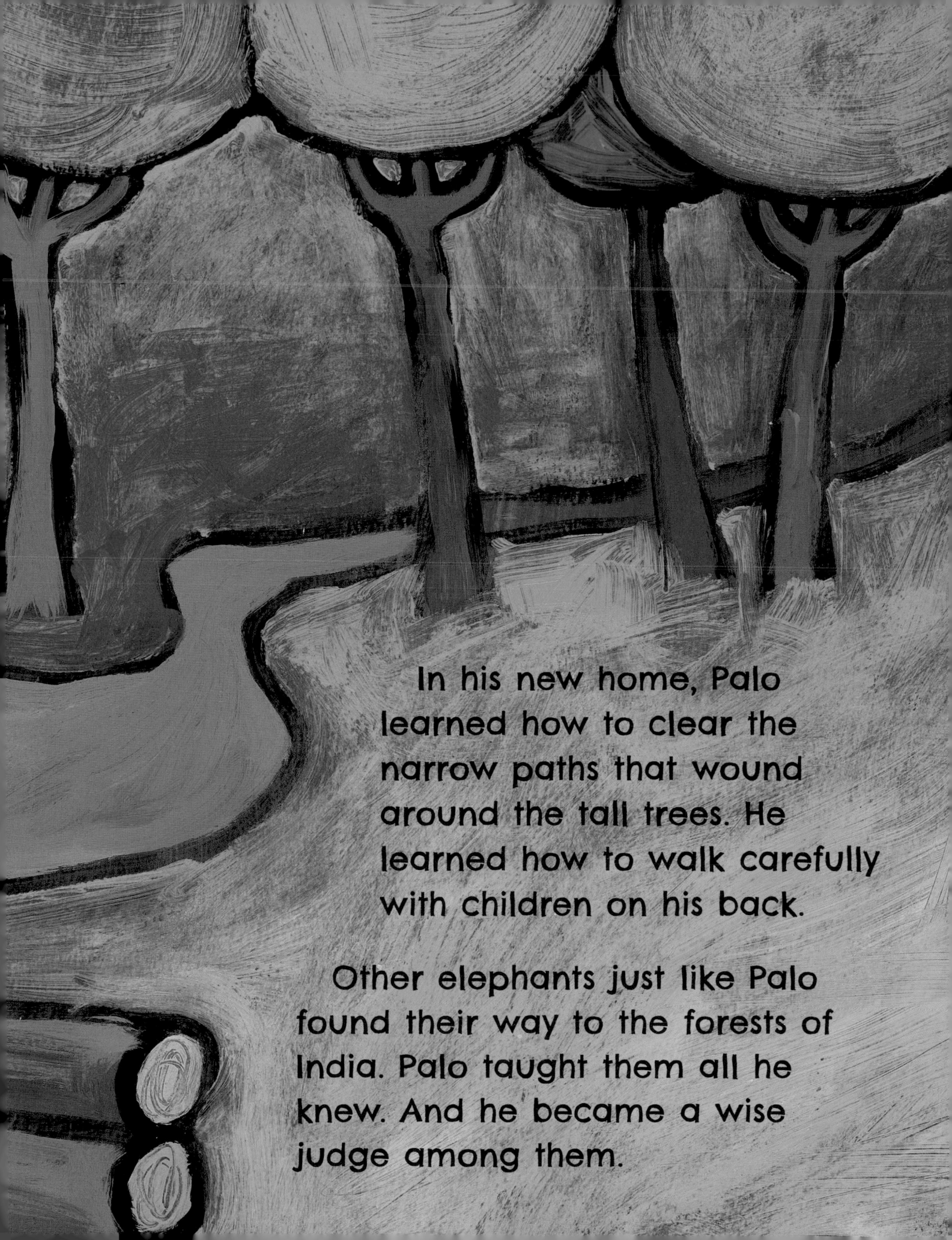

In his new home, Palo learned how to clear the narrow paths that wound around the tall trees. He learned how to walk carefully with children on his back.

Other elephants just like Palo found their way to the forests of India. Palo taught them all he knew. And he became a wise judge among them.

In her new home, Mala learned how to find plenty of food and cool pools of water. At night, she found the safest places to rest. She learned how to protect her calves from the dangers of the plains.

Other elephants just like Mala found
their way to the grasslands of Africa.

Mala taught them all she knew. And
she became a great leader among them.

And that is how the Indian elephant,
with its neat ears and quiet ways,
and the African elephant, with
its grand ears and excitable
ways, found their
homelands.

AFRICAN AND INDIAN ELEPHANTS

Today, African elephants roam in small herds across the grasslands of east, central and southern Africa. The Indian (or Asian) elephant lives in the forests of India and southeast Asia. In the grasslands and forests, both types of elephant gather leaves, bark and branches to eat.

Elephants have a close family life. The herds are made up mostly of females and calves. Male elephants are called bulls. Female elephants in the herd help to look after a mother elephant's calf. African mother elephants flap their huge ears onto their backs to call their children.

An elephant's trunk can pull out small trees. It can carry loads too. It can also be used as a hosepipe — the trunk can suck up water and squirt it into the animal's mouth, or wash down the elephant's back to keep it cool. Inside the trunk, the African elephant has two fingers that can pick up quite small objects. The Indian elephant has one finger. Elephants have a very good sense of smell too.

Near the African elephant's trunk grow two long tusks made of smooth ivory. For hundreds of years, craftsmen have carved this ivory into fine jewelry and ornaments. But to get the ivory tusks, hunters have killed hundreds of thousands of elephants, so the hunting of elephants in Africa has been banned.

The African elephant cannot be tamed, but the Indian elephant can be trained to use its trunk to pick up logs and other goods. It has also been taught how to carry loads on its back. In this way, the Indian elephant works for human beings.

— Catherine Chambers

Barefoot Books, 2067 Massachusetts Ave, Cambridge, MA 02140
Barefoot Books, 29/30 Fitzroy Square, London, W1T 6LQ

Text copyright © 2000 by Catherine Chambers. Illustrations copyright © 2000 by Caroline Mockford. The moral rights of Catherine Chambers and Caroline Mockford have been asserted. First published in Great Britain by Barefoot Books, Ltd and in the United States of America by Barefoot Books, Inc in 2000. This paperback edition first published in 2016. All rights reserved

Graphic design by Barefoot Books. Reproduction by Grafiscan, Italy
Printed in China on 100% acid-free paper
This book was typeset in Chelsea Market Pro and GoudyInfant
The illustrations were prepared in acrylics

ISBN 978-1-78285-282-7

British Cataloguing-in-Publication Data: a catalogue record
for this book is available from the British Library

Library of Congress
Cataloging-in-Publication Data
is available under
LCCN 2007300357

1 3 5 7 9 8 6 4 2